OVER THE SEAS AND FAR AWAY;
SAIL IN A BOAT FOR ALL OF A DAY

The Katie Morag Collection

Containing:

The Big Katie Morag Storybook
and
The Second Katie Morag Storybook

This edition is produced for The Book People Ltd,
Hall Wood Avenue, Haydock, St Helens WA11 9 UL

The Big Katie Morag Storybook first published 1996
Copyright © Mairi Hedderwick 1996

The Second Katie Morag Storybook first published 1998
Copyright © Mairi Hedderwick 1999

Random House UK Limited Reg. No. 954009

A CIP catalogue record for this book is available from the British
Library

Printed in Singapore

The Katie Morag Collection

Mairi Hedderwick

TED SMART

To Mark and Heather who got the drift & Tammie
and Patrick who got the message

THE BIG
KATIE MORAG
STORYBOOK

Mairi Hedderwick

Gertrude Isobel Tilsley (Bel)
(Historian & Crofter)   M.   Capt. Nils J. Olsen
(Helicopter pilot)

GRANNIE
ISLAND

Sven & Sean Olsen (TWINS)
(Singer & Cellist)

Isobel Olsen   M.   Peter McColl
(Post mistress)   (Shopkeeper)

Katie Morag McColl   Liam McColl   Flora Ann McColl

KATIE MORAG

KATIE MORAG'S FAMILY TREE

Grace Margaret Nicol (Meg)
(Retired Nurse & Secretary)

GRANMA MAINLAND

M. Hector Archibald McColl (1)
(Butcher - deceased)

Neilly Beag (2)
(Crofter)

James McColl
(Reverend)

M. Rachel Stoddart

Matthew McColl
(Whereabouts unknown)

Hector McColl

Archie McColl

Dougal McColl

Jamie McColl

Murdo Iain McColl

THE BIG BOY COUSINS

KATIE MORAG'S ISLAND

Katie Morag's island is called the Isle of Struay. Nobody can walk to Katie Morag's island, or take a bus or a train. The only way to go is by boat.

The *Lady of the Isles* comes three times a week bringing all the things the islanders need: letters and parcels, newspapers and magazines, provisions for the shop, supplies for the Struachs. Visitors come that way too.

If it is very stormy no boat comes at all.

"An island is a piece of land with water all around," says the captain of the *Lady of the Isles*.

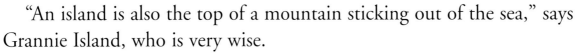

"An island is also the top of a mountain sticking out of the sea," says Grannie Island, who is very wise.

All the islanders have little boats. Little boats must hug the land; big boats can sail far away to distant places. The mainland is very distant. That is where Granma Mainland lives – some of the time.

Granma Mainland is a High-flyer.

Neilly Beag smiles up at the sky. "You *can* go another way to a wee island," he reminds everyone.

"But boats are best," mutters Grannie Island.

Katie Morag smiles. She loves both of her grandmothers just the same.

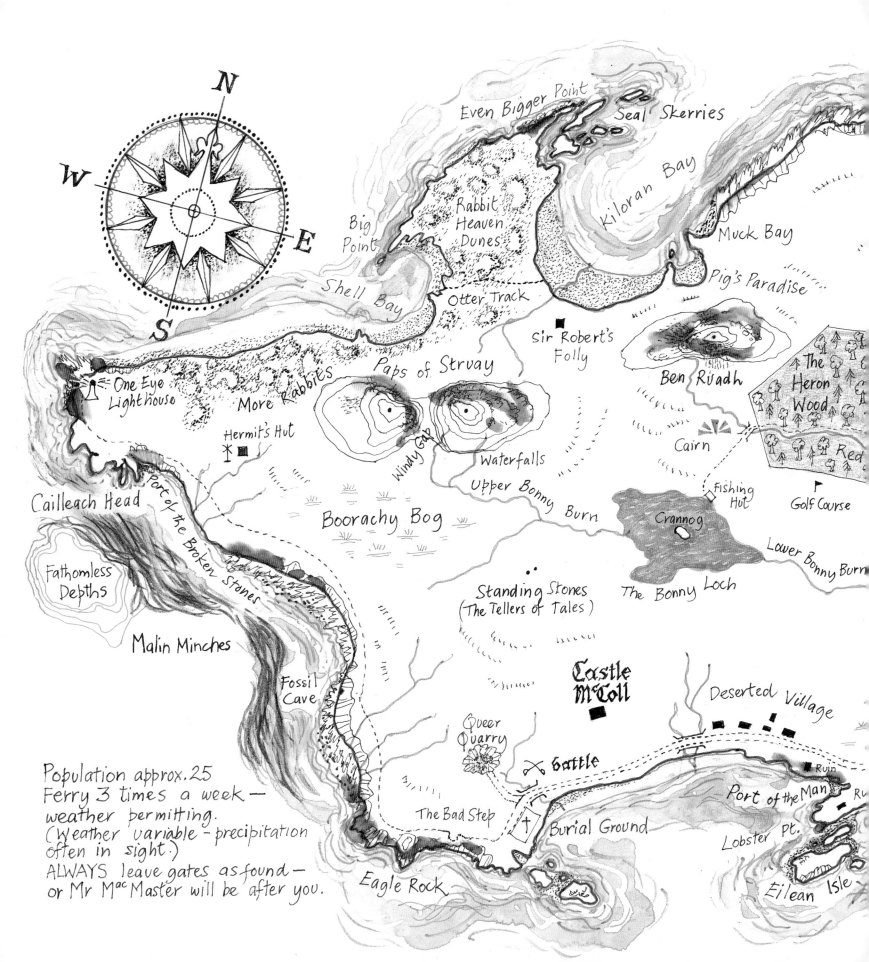

THE ISLE OF STRUAY

Scale: 4 inches to one statute mile

WINDY WEATHER

The West winds blow to Struay Isle;
Smirring rain and clouds the while.

EAST   WEST

The South winds blow and warm the sea;
'Fine to paddle,' say Liam and me.

The East winds blow and nip our ears;
Liam's freezing, close to tears.

HOME's BEST

The North winds blow and we feel snow.
Time for home; it's off we go.

THE BAKING DAY SECRET

Friday is baking day on the Isle of Struay.

That is the day Katie Morag likes to go visiting in the Village. I wonder why?

"Take Liam," said Mrs McColl one particular Friday.

But Katie Morag thought that was a very bad idea.

"I'll keep the bowls for you to lick," her mother promised. Mrs McColl was not a good baker. Licking the bowls was often the best bit of her baking.

Annoyed, Katie Morag pushed Liam towards the first house in the Village. "He'll know my secret now and ALWAYS want to come," she frowned.

The ferryman's wife made quite the most fabbydoo chocolate cakes. "Come to try my new recipe, Katie Morag?" she smiled, as Liam and Katie Morag appeared at the door.

"Oh no!" fibbed Katie Morag. "We've just come to say 'hello'.

Say 'hello' Liam..."

"That's strange," thought the ferryman's wife to herself. Katie Morag always sat down and enjoyed her Friday visits. "Here's a couple of pieces, then, to take home, since you won't have them now," she said in surprise as she put two large slices of cake into a bag. Liam licked his lips.

"Thank you very much," said Katie Morag.

"Want eat!" said Liam, hopefully, when they got outside.

"Certainly NOT!" Katie Morag was firm. Liam must not find out about the Baking Day secret.

Neilly Beag and Granma Mainland were in the next house. What meringues Neilly could bake! Mounds of shiny white spirals sat drying by the stove. The cream for in-between was whipped up stiff.

"Test the best yet, Katie Morag!" he beamed.

"Oh no!" said Katie Morag. "We've just come to say 'hello'!" Katie Morag's mouth was watering.

"That's very odd..." thought Neilly. "Well, you can take some for later, can't you?" he suggested, fetching out a bag.

Maybe it was not so bad Liam coming along, thought Katie Morag. She had never been given *bags* of baking before.

By the time Katie Morag reached the last house in the village, Liam had had to give up his seat in the bogie. Nurse had just finished making syrupy sweet porridgies.

"Perfect timing – have a bite!" Nurse offered the tray.

Of course when Katie Morag refused as usual, Nurse filled yet another bag. Liam was waiting eagerly to take it.

"Want eat NOW!" demanded Liam as they headed homewards, the bogie laden with cake and meringues, doughnuts, shortbread and porridgies.

"NO!" said Katie Morag angrily. She was wondering where she could hide all the bags without Liam seeing.

When the two of them got back home, Katie Morag hid the bogie round the corner of the house. The kitchen of the Shop and Post Office was in a terrible mess. Pots and jugs, spoons and bowls were all over the place.

Burnt biscuits and buns, soggy sunk sponges and leather-hard pancakes were scattered on the table. Mrs McColl was in tears by the sink. The baby was covered in flour.

"The new teacher and his wife are coming to tea," wailed Mrs McColl in despair. "What am I going to give them to eat?"

Katie Morag and Liam looked at each other, reluctantly.

Suddenly, "We've got lots of baking for a scrumptious tea," said Katie Morag.

"How *kind* of the Villagers," sniffed Mrs McColl. "Maybe they'll teach me how to bake one day?"

It did not take long to tidy everything up. The tea party with the new teacher and his wife was a great success. Katie Morag and Liam were very polite and only ate what they were offered. They were so happy to see Mrs McColl happy again.

"What wonderful bakers you islanders are!" praised the new teacher.

"Well, I have a lot to learn," replied Mrs McColl, graciously. She was being very honest, don't you think?

"You are my very best friends!" said Mrs McColl after the visitors had gone. "I think you deserve a special treat! Off to bed, the two of you!"

Katie Morag and Liam looked bewildered – that was no treat...

But it was. One bag of baking had been missed in the rush to tidy the kitchen. It was Nurse's super, syrupy-sweet porridgies. Mrs McColl said they could have them for a midnight feast if they promised to brush their teeth after. They promised.

Katie Morag and Liam never went to bed quicker than on the night of the Baking Day Secret.

Once all the house was quiet and the stars peeping in the window they began their feast by torchlight. They even left some over for the next day. They had to... they were so full.

RECIPE FOR PORRIDGIES

Pre-heat oven to Gas Mark 3 or 300ºF or 110ºC (or when the needle reaches 8 o'clock on Grannie Island's stove).

Grease a 20cm x 30cm (8" x 12") shallow baking tray.

Ingredients:

100g (4oz) butter
75g (3oz) soft brown sugar
30ml (2 tablespoons) syrup
200g (8oz) rolled oats
pinch of salt

Melt butter in a large pan over a low heat.
Add sugar and syrup and salt. Mix well.
Stir in rolled oats. Mix very well.

Spread mixture evenly in tray with palette knife.
Bake for 25-35 minutes, till goldie brown.
Take out of oven. Let cool a little.
Mark in squares or fingers with knife.
Leave in tray till cold. Put
pieces in an airtight tin.

Katie Morag likes them
best when still warm.

TIRESOME TED SEA SHANTIES

KATIE MORAG HAS LOST HER TED

Katie Morag has lost her Ted
And can't tell where to find him.
Leave him alone and he'll come home,
The wind and the tide behind him.

OF ALL THE FISH THAT SWIM IN THE SEA

Of all the fish that swim in the sea,
The Tiresome Ted is the one for me.

A Herring's no use to cuddle in bed;
Cuddle a herring? I'd rather be dead!

Mackerels are slippery, most used for bait,
Some doused in vinegar, six to a plate.

Flounders are flatfish; that everyone knows,
But under the sand they nibble your toes.

Eels have got teeth, sharp set in their jaw.
Down deep a-snaking – is that what I saw?

The Cod is the King and that's no mistake,
But sooner or later he's just plain fishcake.

Of all the fish that swim in the sea,
The Tiresome Ted is the one for me.

WHAT SHALL SHE DO?

What shall she do
With a soaking teddy
Washed up on the seashore?

Hang him on the washline
Till he's fluffy;
Wind and sun together.

Put him by the fireside
Till he's cosy;
In your Grannie's kitchen.

Feed him mince and tatties
Till he's pudgy;
Put him on his potty.

Brush his fur and comb him
Till he's lovely;
In the baby's nightie.

Sing a lullaby song
Till he's sleepy.
Then take him into bed.

TIRESOME
TED
SEA
SHANTIES

GRANNIE ISLAND IS ILL

When Grannie Island took ill Mr and Mrs McColl became very worried. "She can't stay over there all alone," exclaimed her daughter, Mrs McColl. "She'll have to come to us until she gets better."

Mr McColl groaned.

Katie Morag was very sorry that her Grannie was not well but thought it would be great fun having her to stay. "We will read her stories," she told Liam, "and we will sit on her bed."

Immediately Grannie Island heard of these plans she was adamant. "East, West – home's best!" she stated firmly. "Go away! I'll be fine – stop fussing."

This meant that the McColls had to go over to Grannie Island's house on the other side of the bay every day to feed, not only Grannie Island but her dog, the cats, the sheep, the hens, ducks and geese. The animals and birds missed Grannie Island and were awkward.

"You are being awkward too!" scolded Mrs McColl. "How can we get on with running the Shop and Post Office if you behave like this?"

Katie Morag said she would stay and look after Grannie Island. "You are far too young!" snapped Mrs McColl. And that was the end of that.

Then Mrs McColl had an idea. Granma Mainland and Neilly Beag had just come back to the island. "The very person to take care of Grannie Island!" thought the McColls. Granma Mainland had been a nurse in her younger days.

"*Now* can I go to Grannie Island's and help?" pleaded Katie Morag. Katie Morag knew that the two grandmothers did not always get on too well.

"As long as you don't get in the way," said her mother.

Whilst Neilly was spring-cleaning the Village house Granma Mainland was intent on doing the same at Grannie Island's.

"Dreadful mess!" she muttered. "And where is the Hoover and the washing machine?"

Grannie Island did not have such things. Helplessly she watched as Granma Mainland took over her home, fussing and cleaning. The dustbin was soon very full.

But as the days passed Grannie Island began to perk up. It was funny to see Granma Mainland on her hands and knees scrubbing the kitchen floor. She had to take off all her fancy clothes and jewellery. Grannie Island's old slippers did not quite suit her.

And when it came to feeding the animals and birds, that was the funniest thing of all – Granma Mainland in Wellingtons and overalls! Grannie Island peeked out of the bedroom window and laughed until her sides were sore.

This made Granma Mainland very angry and she would come in and plump up Grannie Island's pillows abruptly and give her only *one* biscuit with her cup of tea.

When Granma Mainland was not looking, Katie Morag raided the tin and hid extra biscuits under the mattress.

"Where do all these crumbs come from?" fretted Granma Mainland as she swept under the bed for the umpteenth time.

Katie Morag did all the best things for Grannie Island: reading her stories, drawing pictures, turning the tapes on the cassette, helping with the jigsaw and, best of all, helping to eat up the biscuit and grape supplies.

For the most part, everyone got on well and Grannie Island was definitely improving. Evenings were best when Granma Mainland sat down at last. That was when she put her earrings and her high-heeled shoes back on and chatted lovingly to Neilly Beag on the phone.

Katie Morag would be snug on Grannie Island's bed reading her favourite book and the dog and the cats were finally allowed into the house – if their paws were clean.

KATIE MORAG DELIVERS THE MAIL

It was a time of rainbows on the island. The McColls came over one shimmery Sunday to see how everyone was getting on. Grannie Island was back on her feet. The animals and birds were happy again. Granma Mainland was resting on the couch, filing her hard-worked nails and massaging her ankles. Grannie Island's house was spotless.

"There is gold at the end of the rainbow," Katie Morag told Liam as they played outside. "I wish we could find it, don't you?" But no matter how fast they ran they could not catch the rainbow's end. It always moved on – up over the Lady Artist's chimney pot, past the McMasters' stable, through Mrs Bayview's greenhouse, into the deepest part of the Bonny Loch and then far out to sea.

Mrs McColl called them in for tea.

"Grannie Island says she is quite better now. You and Liam can stay with her tonight. We'll take Granma Mainland back to the Village."

Grannie Island thanked Granma Mainland for all her help. She was being polite. Grannie Island actually hated Granma Mainland's fancy cooking, and even more, all her tidying.

What a good mood Grannie Island was in after the McColls and Granma Mainland left.
"Now let's get everything back in its place," she smiled.

The dog and the cats were let in immediately and leapt to their favourite cushions. Katie
Morag and Liam loved setting out all the odds and ends that Granma Mainland had
swept away into boxes and bags.

At supper time they all feasted on mince and tatties and mashed tumshie. "Can't stand
that tagliatelle stuff of Granma Mainland's – slides all over the plate," said Grannie Island.

Next morning, Katie Morag and Liam packed their rucksacks. It was time to go. Much as Katie Morag had enjoyed being at Grannie Island's, she looked forward to going home.

"Where are my old photos?" Grannie Island was still searching. "My favourite one is missing!" she wailed.

"Here comes Granma Mainland!" called Katie Morag from the open door, relieved. "She'll know..."

"I don't want that woman in my house ever again!" shouted Grannie Island. "Bossing and losing my things..."

But Granma Mainland was not in a bossy mood. She was very, very upset. "I've lost my favourite and most expensive gold earrings. They must be here!"

She stood, aghast, at the returned chaos of Grannie Island's house. "I'll never find them in all this mess! How could you?"

Katie Morag and Liam thought it best to get out of the house until the two grandmothers had calmed down and, hopefully, found their precious possessions.

Another rainbow appeared in the sky. It was very close; so close, in fact, that the end of it was definitely in Grannie Island's dustbin. This time Katie Morag and Liam moved like lightning head-first into the bin before the rainbow disappeared.

Gold *did* glitter in amongst the rubbish... Granma Mainland's earrings! And underneath the rest of the junk, the box of old photos! There was also a brightly knitted tea cosy that Liam fancied for a hat and a tiny little wooden horse that Katie Morag knew would love to sit on her window-sill.

Cries of delight met Katie Morag and Liam as they raced, rather grubbily, into the house with the rainbow treasures.

The two grandmothers apologised to each other and, of course, Grannie Island said Katie Morag and Liam could keep the hat and the horse.

Once Grannie Island had put her favourite photo back on the jam-packed sideboard she walked everyone along the road a bit before saying "Goodbye" and "Thank you".

Granma Mainland's earrings glinted in the sun as she turned to wave. Katie Morag and Liam waved too and then everyone headed homeward, their precious possessions safe and sound.

But Katie Morag's most special possession was knowing that she and Liam had caught the rainbow's end.

THE CATS OF STRUAY

Scratch Patch is the mother of them all.
She *loves* having kittens just because...

Haggis Virginia *sleeps* on the hamster cage
– just in case...

Justeenie loves Big Cat – just teenie, of course...

Jake is the thief – isn't that JUST awful?

Mr Mistake is – just a mistake...

Freddie is *FEROCIOUS* – just as well...

FaBbyDoo is a mouser – just in time?

Pussy Willow is a knitter – just for fun...

Charlie is the purrer – just to please...

And Seamus is the father of them all – just because...

SUMMER VISITORS

Many visitors come on holiday to the island in the summer. Katie Morag's mother and father are forever emptying boxes and stacking shelves, polishing the counter and fussing around the Holiday People. Katie Morag gets very bored.

One summer, Mrs McColl decided to make a fancy arrangement in the shop window for the visitors to admire.

"Go down to the shore, Katie Morag, for some sand and seaweed. Just to add the finishing touch," said Mrs McColl as she stacked a pyramid of beach-balls under an archway of buckets and spades. "And anything else that would look good," she added.

Katie Morag shovelled a layer of sand and then a layer of seaweed into her bogie. She scanned the tide line. Further along the shore there was something strange. Dark and shiny, it looked like a wet rumpled jacket; but it was moving. The sleeve bit was waving at her. Katie Morag was more interested than frightened. What could have been buttons seemed more like eyes and, sure enough, when Katie Morag got closer the buttons blinked.

"A baby seal!" cried Katie Morag. She looked out to sea. The mother must be hunting for fish in the bay. Katie Morag looked long and hard. But no head bobbed up out of the waves to check all was well with the pup.

The seal pup stared at Katie Morag with large appealing eyes.

"You would look very good in the seaside display!" thought Katie Morag. Suddenly the shop was an exciting place to be, "I'll look after you," said Katie Morag. "I'll call you Ròn."

"Take that seal back where he belongs!" exclaimed Mrs McColl. "He is most definitely NOT going in my window display!"

Before she could say more, Ròn with a heave on his flippers, lurched from the bogie on to the window shelf. Buckets and spades and balls went in all directions.

Mrs McColl was furious.

Katie Morag raced down the brae to catch the bouncing balls and bumped into the Holiday Children. They said they would help her take the seal pup back.

Katie Morag had a heavy heart as she pushed Ròn down to the water's edge. He flippered away into the sea. No mother came to meet him, within minutes he was back at Katie Morag's feet. She tried again to shove him off but the same thing happened again. Back he came! Her new friends cheered.

"We'll just have to look after you ourselves, then!" said Katie Morag, delighted with Ròn's return.

They sneaked him into the shed when no one was looking and got lots more seaweed for a bed. Mr McColl's barrel of salt herring was very convenient.

Feeding Ròn was difficult. He did not like the Ferryman's wife's chocolate cake but he scoffed left-over fish fingers from Katie Morag's tea, no bother at all. But Katie Morag didn't have fish fingers for tea every day. Soon the barrel of salt herring was empty.

"He eats an *awful* lot," said Jake.

"And he's not toilet trained," sniffed Jemma, "is he?"

"Well no..." agreed Katie Morag, wondering. Katie Morag was worried about the empty barrel but *most* worried about Ròn.

She and the Holiday Children tried dangling their fishing lines over the edge of the old pier but nobody caught anything.

"There are lots of fish in the sea," moaned Katie Morag, "but we are no good at catching them. I bet Ròn could though, if he really tried."

This time when Katie Morag pushed Ròn into the sea they all shouted and yelled when he came back. They banged bits of driftwood together and waved flags of torn netting. The seal looked a bit surprised but, eventually, he turned and headed out for the deep sea where the best fishes live.

Katie Morag was glad Ròn had gone home. She climbed slowly back up the brae to the shop and the Post Office.

"Can my friends come in for tea?" she asked.

"Of course!" said Mrs McColl.

"As long as they don't eat as much as Ròn..." smiled Mr McColl.

TOURIST INFORMATION

YOU
ARE
HERE

That night before she went to bed Katie Morag looked out of her window. She was sure she saw Ròn's head in the bay – or was it a beach-ball?

GOING AWAY FROM STRUAY ISLE;
BACK I'LL COME SAILING IN A WEE WHILE

For Sophie, Sam and Ewan; Fabbydo and Mr. Mistake

THE SECOND
KATIE MORAG
STORYBOOK

Mairi Hedderwick

Katie Morag McColl lives on the Isle of Struay. Her home is up above the Shop and Post Office.

The McColl family live in the busiest part of the island – the Village.

It can be very busy in the Village. Especially on the days that the big boat comes from the mainland bringing the mail, provisions and travellers wanting to visit the island.

Sometimes it can be very noisy in the Village. Especially when the Ferryman and his wife have a late night ceilidh. Neilly Beag lives next door. He so likes the quiet life. That's when he bangs on the wall in

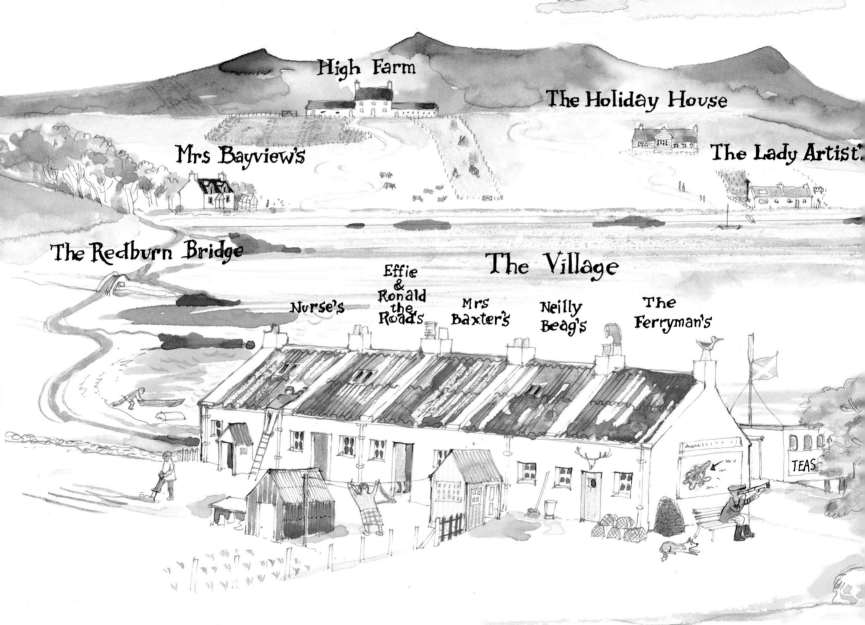

High Farm

The Holiday House

Mrs Bayview's

The Lady Artist's

The Redburn Bridge

The Village

Effie & Ronald the Roads

Nurse's

Mrs Baxter's

Neilly Beag's

The Ferryman's

TEAS

between and shouts, "Shut up! Shut up! It's time you were in your beds!"

On the other side of the Bay all the houses are far apart and peaceful. If anyone has a rowdy party it does not matter – there are no neighbours close by to disturb.

In the last house at the end of the road lives Grannie Island. She loves having parties.

First thing in the morning and last thing at night Katie Morag looks out of her bedroom window over to Grannie Island's house. "Good morning, Grannie Island," she calls. "Goodnight, Grannie Island!" she whispers.

THE ISLE of STRUAY

Grannie's

The Mainland

The New Pier

The Jetty

ISLE of STRUAY SHOP & POST OFFICE

OBAN TIMES GET YOUR COPY HERE

BISTRO

TO THE NEW PIER

WELCOME

WEST HIGHLAND FREE PRESS ORDER NOW

The Shop & Post Office

When Katie Morag is in a good mood her bedroom looks like this:

When Katie Morag is in a bad mood THIS is what her bedroom looks like:
"This room is a MIDDEN!" shrieks Mrs McColl.

The Hermit's Hut

Mr McColl's bad moods were always at the end of the month. Not only had he to do all the accounts for the Isle of Struay Shop and Post Office, he also had to visit his brother, Matthew, who lived on the other side of the island.

Mrs McColl refused to visit her brother-in-law.

Matthew was a hermit and lived in a hut. "That hut is just like a midden inside!" exclaimed Mrs McColl. "Decent folks don't live like that!"

Matthew never came to the Village, or at least the last time he had come was so long ago nobody was sure it had ever happened. Everyone came to the Village on boat days. "Even hermits, sometimes," exclaimed the islanders, "to get supplies, surely?"

Katie Morag knew what a hermit was. It was someone who didn't like people around and didn't like going anywhere. And hermits always lived on their own, but in a different way from Grannie Island. Grannie Island lived all alone but she was forever having friends and visitors in and out of her house and popping over to the Village on her old grey tractor to see the McColls at the Shop and Post Office.

All Matthew wanted was to be left alone and to keep his whereabouts unknown. Mr McColl, however, said it was his duty to go once a month and check that his brother was all right.

At the end of this particular month the weather was wet and windy. Mr McColl put on his walking boots and groaned.

Katie Morag and Liam had had to play inside all that morning on account of the weather and now they were very bored with each other. When Katie Morag gets fed up with people she likes to be on her own. She gets her paints out and then forgets all the horrible things that have happened.

When Liam gets fed up he loves to pester and PESTER his big sister . . .

"Go AWAY!" screamed Katie Morag, as Liam emptied all the stickle bricks over her sheet of paper and smudged the wet paint.

"WHAT IS GOING ON?" Mrs McColl was in a bad mood too. "This room is a MIDDEN!" she shrieked. "What am I going to do with you? What a worry you are! Get it tidy AT ONCE! And then, you, Katie Morag," she added, "put your boots on and go over to Matthew's with your father."

"I bet no one tells Uncle Matthew to tidy up his room and I bet he's got no wee brother who spoils everything," thought Katie Morag, angrily.

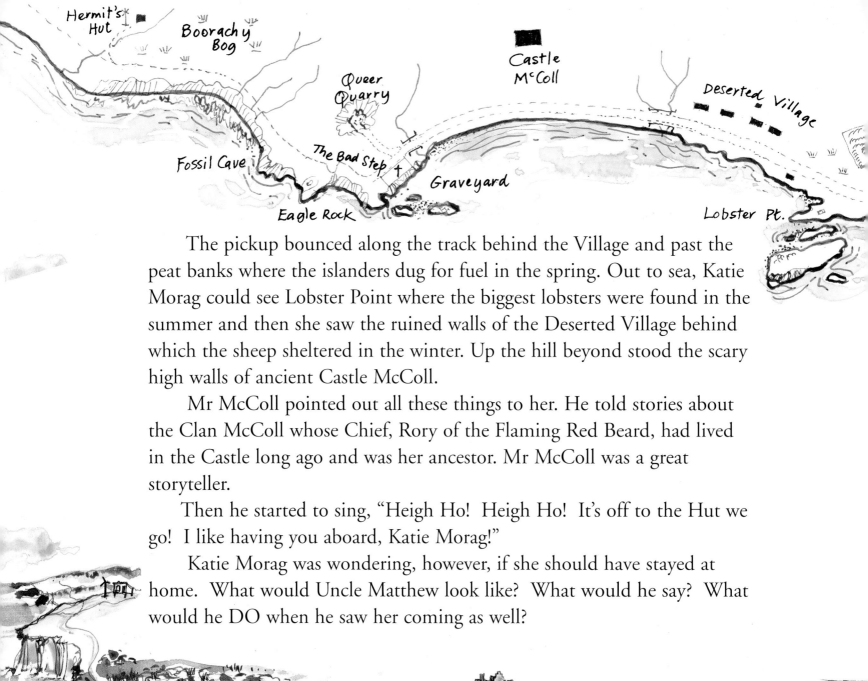

The pickup bounced along the track behind the Village and past the peat banks where the islanders dug for fuel in the spring. Out to sea, Katie Morag could see Lobster Point where the biggest lobsters were found in the summer and then she saw the ruined walls of the Deserted Village behind which the sheep sheltered in the winter. Up the hill beyond stood the scary high walls of ancient Castle McColl.

Mr McColl pointed out all these things to her. He told stories about the Clan McColl whose Chief, Rory of the Flaming Red Beard, had lived in the Castle long ago and was her ancestor. Mr McColl was a great storyteller.

Then he started to sing, "Heigh Ho! Heigh Ho! It's off to the Hut we go! I like having you aboard, Katie Morag!"

Katie Morag was wondering, however, if she should have stayed at home. What would Uncle Matthew look like? What would he say? What would he DO when he saw her coming as well?

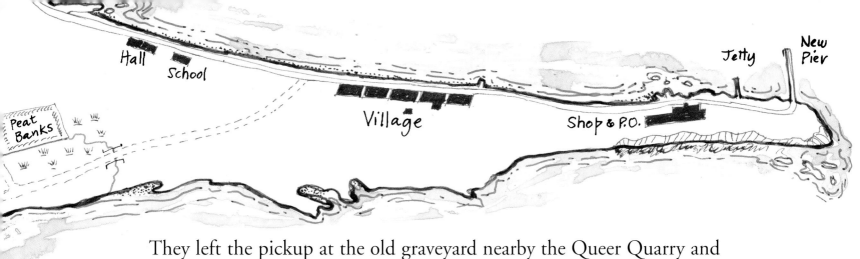

Hall
School
Peat Banks
Village
Shop & P.O.
Jetty
New Pier

They left the pickup at the old graveyard nearby the Queer Quarry and started to scramble up and over the Bad Step, past the Fossil Cave way down deep below the cliffs that looked out to sea over the Fathomless Depths.

When they got to the Boorachy Bog, Katie Morag was very glad of her Wellington boots. It was an adventurous journey.

They were getting nearer and nearer to the Hermit's Hut. Soon they were there.

Mrs McColl was all wrong. Admittedly, the inside of the Hut was very full and cluttered and a cockerel was standing on top of a pile of dishes in the sink but it could never be called a midden. Everything looked very interesting even though half of it was on the floor. "Highest shelf in the house," Mrs McColl always said. But it made sense to Katie Morag – much easier to find things that way.

"Matthew! You are a slovenly disgrace to the McColl family!" cried Mr McColl, shaking his head at his brother. "What am I going to do with you? What a worry you are!"

"I don't worry about you," replied Matthew quietly. He saw Katie Morag peeking behind her father's back.

"What do you think, Katie Morag?"

Uncle Matthew was nothing like Katie Morag remembered, or imagined she remembered. He did look a bit strange with straggly scruffy hair over his eyes. But she often looked like that. He spoke very gently and he wasn't going to DO anything awful – that was obvious.

He was very pre-occupied.

On the table were lots of brushes and pots of colours and all around, the walls – the actual walls – were covered with pictures showing all the things that Katie Morag had seen on the journey that afternoon. Mrs McColl would never allow her to do that on her bedroom wall...

"I think you like being on your own," she answered, bravely. She understood.

Whilst Mr McColl shooed out the cockerel Uncle Matthew took Katie Morag into his garden. Strawberries were fat and juicy on their stalks. Raspberries and loganberries swelled from branches. Apples and pears groaned from trees. Every variety of fruit and vegetable was there for the picking. Honey bees buzzed in and out of hives and the cockerel's hens laid more eggs than they could cope with. A brown and white goat popped her head over the fence.

Of course Matthew didn't have to go to the Village for supplies!

And there was the real midden. It was very tidy. The cockerel was atop, showing off.

Matthew went back into the Hut smiling a special goodbye smile to Katie Morag. Her pockets were full of strawberries.

"I would like to visit Uncle Matthew again," she told her dad as they set off homewards...

Mr McColl smiled. "I think that would be very fine," he replied. "I'm going to help him with his wall painting. I'll paint you and me walking along the cliffs above the Fossil Cave." Katie Morag was excited.

Perhaps it wasn't so bad having a hermit in the family after all.

"I think Uncle Matthew is magic and I think it is best that his whereabouts are unknown," stated Katie Morag.

She looked forward to the end of next month. And the next. Not only would she see Uncle Matthew again, she would also have her dad all to herself on the long journey over to the Hermit's Hut. It had been a great day after all.

Everyone grows something on the Isle of Struay. Well, nearly everyone...

Mrs Bayview wins the prize at the Show for the greatest variety of flowers. Sometimes Mrs Bayview gets lost in her garden. So do her tools.

Mr McMaster, the farmer at High Farm, says a garden is far too small for him. He plants fields and fields of tatties and turnips, cabbages and carrots. He has to make sure the fences are strong.

The Lady Artist has a sculpture garden. The sculptures don't grow but my, the grass certainly does!

Neilly Beag has a window box. In it he grows chives and parsley, fennel and mint, thyme, camomile, lavender and rosemary. Neilly Beag chops herbs into his soups and stews. And his teapot.

Katie Morag, quite contrary
How does your garden grow?
With cockle shells and silver bells
And pretty maids all in a row!

Dainty cowries, clams and mussels
No need to weed or mow!
No aching back or blistered hands
It's off to the shore I go!

Someone hasn't been on the sand – yet!
I wonder who?

Castle McColl

Katie Morag McColl's two cats spend most of their time sleeping and stretching, comfy and cuddly on the top of Katie Morag's bed. When the moon is full, however, they go wandering. For days and nights. No one knows where they go. They like it that way. Eventually, with the aid of the great full moon they find their way home.

Fabbydoo is large and a golden gingery red colour. Mr Mistake is smaller and pure white all over. He has one poor eye that can't see a thing but Fabbydoo looks after him. They are great friends.

But not with the Big Boy Cousins. When the Big Boy Cousins come for their holidays to the island they tease Fabbydoo and Mr Mistake. The cats jump off the cosy cushions and hope that the moon is full.

"Here they come! Hide! Hide!" Katie Morag warned Fabbydoo and Mr Mistake one day. The boat had arrived with all the holiday people and there were the Cousins disembarking with their camping gear.

As long as her cats were hiding safe, Katie Morag loved it when the Big Boy Cousins came to stay. They pitched their tent at Grannie Island's and Katie Morag was allowed to take her sleeping bag over and camp too. It was good knowing that Grannie was nearby – especially in the middle of the night.

"It's different this time," declared Hector, the biggest Boy Cousin. "We are pitching the tent by the Castle! It's boring over at Grannie Island's."

What Hector really meant was that the usual site was too close to Grannie Island. There she could keep too much of an eye on them. Once Katie Morag and the Big Boy Cousins got together they got up to all sorts of mischief.

"Please can I go? PLEASE!" Katie Morag implored her parents.

Castle McColl was a long way away from the Village. "Oh! All right," said her father. "As long as you promise to tell them all about Clan Chief Rory McColl of the Flaming Red Beard and the Wee White One-Eyed Ghost..."

The Big Boy Cousins could have done without Katie Morag dragging behind and maybe getting homesick in the middle of the night, but stories about Clan Chief Rory McColl and the Wee White One-Eyed Ghost sounded interesting.

After all, they were McColls, too...

Castle McColl was ancient. Nobody had lived in it for years and years. Just the pigeons, the mice and a bat or two. Long ago it had been a lively place full of chieftains and warriors, maidens, servants and deerhounds. And the Clan Chief Rory of the Flaming Red Beard. And the Wee White One-Eyed Ghost – if Mr McColl was to be believed...

It was very exciting to pitch the tent beside such history, said Hector, pompously, as everyone busied themselves setting up camp. Katie Morag helped Jamie gather old timber from the Castle for the fire. He wanted to hear the stories about the Castle straight away.

"No!" said Katie Morag, a bit bossily. "Once we have had our supper and it is time to go to bed. THAT is the time for stories..." She enjoyed knowing something the others did not.

"Bedtime stories! Pah!" sneered Hector after they had gorged on sausages and beans, Grannie Island's apple pie and gallons of juice. Hector was a bit bad-tempered. There hadn't been enough sausages. He was sure some were missing.

"Yeah! said Archie. "Try catching me going to bed! I'm going to stay up all night!" The cousins cheered and raced off into the empty gloomy Castle, except for Jamie who felt a bit sorry for Katie Morag and stayed behind.

"Come and tell us the stories in HERE! Katie Morag," the others teased and taunted, through the arrow slit windows.

Katie Morag wasn't sure about that. Maybe neither was Jamie. They both wished Grannie Island was nearby. It was beginning to get dark. A big cheesy full moon was coming up over the sea. The glow from the campfire was warm and the sleeping bags in the tent were looking so cosy...

But she wasn't going to let the Big Boy Cousins – or Jamie – know she was frightened.

"Come on!" she said to Jamie and ran as fast as she could into the Castle.

The Big Boy Cousins were hiding, calling with echoey voices from shadowy corners, "Yoo Whoo-oo! Yoo Whoo-oo! Katie Morag and Jamie are afraid of Big Chief Flaming Red Beard and the Wee White One-Eyed Ghost! Fearties! Fearties!"

"We are NOT!" shouted back Katie Morag, riled. "Ready or not, we're coming to get you!"

Everything went silent. The Castle was very scary and eerie. The light coming in through the tiny windows was dim... Katie Morag and Jamie held hands and crept the long length of the corridor, their other hands feeling the way along the slimy walls.

Suddenly there was a shrieking and yelling and a blubbering from above. Hector, Archie, Dougal and Murdo Iain came stumbling and clattering down the spiral staircase, terrified out of their wits.

"The Beard! The Beard! It's cut off and it's growling!" screamed Hector as he flew past, heading for the entrance to the Castle.

"And the Wee White One-Eyed Ghost is up there too – just staring and staring with its one eye!" yelled Archie.

Just as Katie Morag and Jamie were turning round to flee for their lives as well, Katie Morag heard the growling.

She recognised it.

Letting go of Jamie's tugging hand she found her way up the darkening staircase to the room above. There in a shadowy corner WAS a big gingery red hairy lump of a thing, very like a cut-off beard. And it WAS growling...

It was Fabbydoo chewing his way through a string of sausages!!

Fabbydoo always growls when he is happy. So does Mr Mistake. So guess who was the Wee White One-Eyed Ghost staring and staring, waiting patiently for his share?

"Oh! Fabbydoo and Mr Mistake, aren't you wonderful!" whispered Katie Morag, giving them each a cuddle. "See you back home at the end of the full moon – and the camping holiday!" Then she carefully found her way down the dark stairs and along the even darker corridor to the outside of the Castle. The dark blue sky was full of stars.

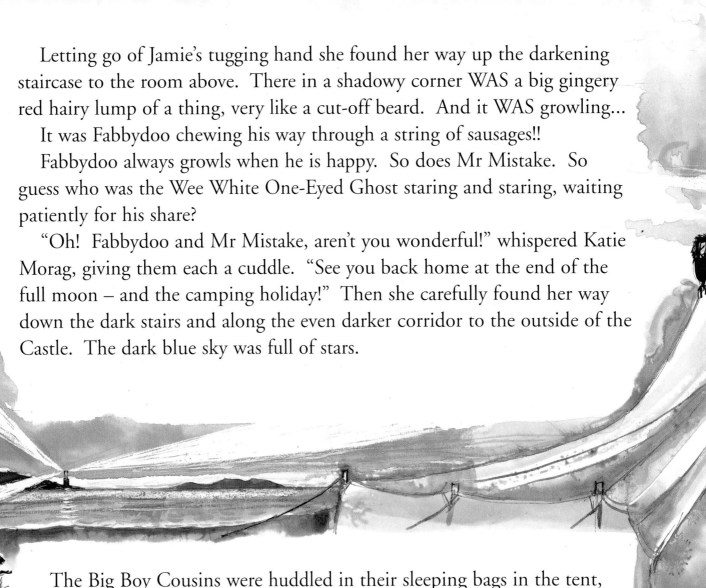

The Big Boy Cousins were huddled in their sleeping bags in the tent, still terrified by their experience, amazed at Katie Morag's bravery. She decided not to tell them about Fabbydoo and Mr Mistake.

"Now it's time for bedtime stories," she said.

"No thank you!" replied the Big Boy Cousins, scaredly, and rolled over to sleep.

Katie Morag sat for a while looking out of the tent flap at the moon, the stars and the silhouette of Castle McColl before she snuggled down to sleep. She could hear Mr Mistake's growl... Good, she thought, it was his turn now to get a share of the sausages.

Then she thought she might tell Jamie in the morning about the real Flaming Red Beard and the real Wee White One-Eyed Ghost. But only if he could keep the secret...

Castle McColl

Castle McColl is an ancient place of ancient stones and ancient bones. Far and away the WORSTEST place — DON'T go in! DON'T GO IN! Through the black dark creaking door there are corridor horrors with fungal balungals and slime slafalime. It's terrible scerrible and slugawful slippery; it's bugawful squashery, and bat-awful squeakery. It's spidery crydery - all in your hair! Hidery! Hidery! There are ghosts whoo-whoo-hooing up the stairs and rats a'rastussing down below!

THE TEAM

TEAM

RUN! RUN!

The Tent

The night is coming in from the sea
And we should be home for our tea.
The night is crawling up o'er the moor
And we should be in bed for sure.

The night is creeping right round the tent
Canvassy shadows all bent.
Tie the flap, quickly! Tummies are sickly!
The night is screeping right round the tent!

But the night is outside and we are in here
No claw fingered ghouls for us to fear.
Six torches shine brightly,
Ten hands hold tightly;

THE NIGHT IS OUTSIDE AND
WE ARE SAFE HERE!

Five Boy Cousins

There are five Boy Cousins sitting on the wall,
And if one Boy Cousin should accidentally fall,
There'd be four Boy Cousins sitting on the wall.

Four Boy Cousins sitting on the wall,
And if one Boy Cousin should accidentally fall,
There'd be three Boy Cousins sitting on the wall.

Three Boy Cousins sitting on the wall,
And if one Boy Cousin should accidentally fall,
There'd be two Boy Cousins sitting on the wall.

Two Boy Cousins sitting on the wall,
And if one Boy Cousin should accidentally fall,
THERE'D BE ME AND MURDO IAIN
SITTING ON THE WALL!

Pussy Cats

Pussy cats, Pussy cats,
Where have you been?
We've been a'hunting
But n'er to be seen.

Pussy cats, Pussy cats,
What did you catch?
We caught out the Cousins;
WE won the match!

The Day of the Birthdays

Katie Morag has such a big family. Some of the family live on the island; someone on the mainland; and some in faraway countries. Katie Morag can't work out if this is a good thing or a bad thing. Especially when it comes to birthdays.

"The bigger the family, the more cards and presents you get on YOUR birthday," she explained to her wee brother Liam. "But then, think," she added ruefully, "of all the cards and presents you have to GIVE... AND I have to share my birthday..."

"Birdie Peasants!" smiled Liam, holding up his hands.

"Oh! WHY do I bother to talk to him," Katie Morag thought to herself. "He just doesn't UNDERSTAND."

Liam has a birthday all to himself in September. Katie Morag has her birthday in May. AND SO DO BOTH OF HER GRANDMOTHERS! Would you believe it? All three of them. On the exact same day! Imagine that!

Now this can be a really good thing – or a really bad thing...

Ever since Christmas Katie Morag had been counting the days until her birthday.

"And you'd better count the pennies in your piggybank," Mrs McColl reminded her. "What are you going to get for Grannie Island and Granma Mainland?"

There were no special shops on the Isle of Struay. Just the Shop and Post Office which only sold food and essentials like mousetraps and buckets and fishing line. Not very exciting for birthday presents. And not at all secret. Everyone knew what was on every shelf of the Shop and Post Office.

Katie Morag loved looking through the big mainland store catalogue.

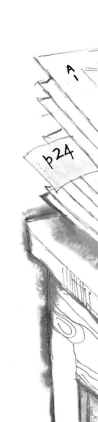

She knew exactly what she wanted for her birthday. There it was on page 24. She had circled a big red felt tip pen circle around the order number. And if anyone wanted to give her anything else she had marked that too on page 51. Then there was a third best present if the big store had run out of the first two. That was on page 109. A fourth best was marked, just in case. And a fifth. But that would be asking too much.

The items had been chosen months ago. The catalogue was well thumbed.

Mrs McColl reminded Katie Morag again, "All our orders will have to be posted today if everything is to come on the boat in time. Hurry up! Choose your presents for Grannie Island and Granma Mainland."

Katie Morag ordered a packet of nails for Grannie Island; Grannie Island was very practical. She ordered a bottle of perfume for Granma Mainland; Granma Mainland liked smelling good. Grannie Island said this was going to be a special birthday for her because she was going to be a special age.

"How old is that?" asked Katie Morag.

"As old as my pinkie finger and a little bit older than my teeth," Grannie Island answered and would say no more.

"I'm going to give a party," she continued, "to everyone on the island. Granma Mainland is coming. The three of us will have a great day and so will everyone else!"

Katie Morag wondered if Grannie Island had noticed the red circles in the catalogue. And what about Granma Mainland?

Weeks before her birthday Katie Morag went down to the pier every boatday and asked the Captain if there were any parcels for her. Of course she was hoping for the presents she had ordered for the two grandmothers but secretly she was hoping to see the size of parcel addressed to Mr and Mrs McColl. Then she'd know if they had looked at page 24 of the catalogue. That was definitely the biggest present. She would know by its shape.

But nothing came.

"Don't fret, Katie Morag," said Mr McColl. "There's time enough yet." And he went back to stocking the shelves of the Shop and Post Office. "Looks as if I'm running out of flour and sugar," he noticed. "Need to get the boat to bring more."

The week before the Birthdays, Granma Mainland arrived. That was fun! Granma Mainland shared Katie Morag's bedroom and let Katie Morag try on all her make-up. "Sorry there is no perfume," she apologised. "I have quite run out!"

Katie Morag was delighted but didn't say why.

Katie Morag decided it was just as wonderful choosing presents for other people as choosing them for yourself. It gave you a tickly feeling inside. She couldn't wait until the day of the Birthdays. Grannie Island would be so pleased with her present too.

And then everything went wrong. Nobody's parcels came to the island.

A wild rogue storm blew up the day before the Birthdays and the boat could not tie up at the pier on account of the giant waves. "Too dangerous!" shouted the Captain. "The forecast is not good. It will be next week before I get back." And his voice faded away under the howl of the wind and the boat disappeared into the frothing waves with all the parcels still aboard.

"No presents for the Birthdays!" Katie Morag was in tears.

"No point in having a party!" Grannie Island was miserable.

The islanders went slowly back up the hill from the pier. All of them very disappointed, although they knew, as did Katie Morag, that the presents and the party would happen for sure when the storm came to an end. But the actual Birthdays the next day were going to be so sad without...

"Birdie peasants?" Liam was trying to understand what was going on.

"Oh! SHUT UP, Liam, PLEASE!" Katie Morag was sitting on the edge of her bed, snivelling.

She had been so looking forward to getting her presents but she was just as excited at the thought of seeing her grandmothers' faces when they saw THEIR presents.

"Birdie peasants!" Liam said again, firmly, pushing his favourite toy onto her lap.

Katie Morag realised she was being horrid to her wee brother. And then she realised something else. "Liam! You are just brilliant!" she said, giving him a hug. "I don't need to wait for the boat to come. I'll *make* presents for Grannie Island and Granma Mainland! And we *will* have a party!"

She knew she would not be able to make nails for Grannie Island. You needed a big factory for that. But she remembered something that Grannie Island had said about her special birthday. She rummaged in Mrs McColl's sewing bag and picked out Grannie Island's favourite colours – blues and greens and lemony yellows. With great care and patience she plaited together the shiny threads until the length could go tightly round two of her fingers and just a bit more. Then she cut the threads and tied the ends together in a neat little bow.

"Wha'sit?" asked Liam. He was being exceptionally good and not interfering with what Katie Morag was doing.

"Wait and see," said Katie Morag as she wrapped the delicate circle of threads in her best hankie.

Next she got an empty yoghurt tub and its top from the make-do box. She took it to the bathroom and, choosing the stripey toothpaste, squeezed a smiley face with the toothpaste on the inside of the top, put the tub on as the lid and wrote on the side FOR GRANNIE ISLAND'S TEETH.

For Grannie Island's Teeeth

It was time for Liam's bath so she got out of the bathroom fast.

"Where are you going?" called Mrs McColl as Katie Morag scuttled across to her bedroom to find her second-best hankie. "Don't be long – it's your turn next."

Katie Morag was already rushing out of the door of the Shop and Post Office. Oh! There was so little time! She had made Grannie Island's present but now for Granma Mainland's.

"Neilly Beag! Neilly Beag! Please can I have a bunch of lavender? I need to make perfume!"

Everyone on the Village street opened their doors, the banging was so loud. Not only did Katie Morag get the lavender from Neilly Beag, but also bags of rose petals once he knew she was making a present for Granma Mainland. "My sweet wee Bobby Dazzler," smiled Neilly Beag, who was very fond of his dear wife.

On the way home Katie Morag took an empty bottle of lemonade from the crate outside the Shop and Post Office. She stuffed the scrunched-up lavender and petals inside. It took ages. It was going to be a *very* big bottle of perfume for wee Granma Mainland!

She could hear Mrs McColl calling, "Katie Morag! Where are you?" from the bathroom.

The great thing about having a wee brother, Katie Morag thought as she lay in the bath, was that you had the bath to yourself whilst he was being dried and changed. She filled the lemonade bottle up with sweet-smelling bath water and wrapped it in a towel – one of Mrs McColl's best.

"Sleep well, Katie Morag – and don't worry about tomorrow. We'll save the birthdays till next week," soothed Mrs McColl once Katie Morag was in bed.

Katie Morag pretended to go to sleep but she had lots more to do. The Birthday cards! Just as important.

The presents and the cards she safely stowed away under her bed.

Then Katie Morag pinned a notice onto the door of her bedroom which said:

THE DAY OF THE BIRTHDAYS
COME AND GET YOUR PRESENTS
GRANNIE ISLAND AND GRANMA MAINLAND!
PARTY IN MY ROOM TO FOLLOW

Signed

Katie Morag

She was quite, quite exhausted and fell asleep within seconds after all the effort.

Next morning Katie Morag woke to all the family standing round her bed chanting, "Happy Birthday, Lazybones!" (Well, to be honest, Liam said "Hattie Birdie, Layzeezones!")

They all had parcels in their hands – Mr and Mrs McColl and the two Grandmothers. So had Liam. The parcels were the shapes of all the things that Katie Morag had circled in the catalogue that she knew so well. And there was even one extra from the Baby.

"Wait! Wait! Before I open my parcels," she mumbled through sleepy eyes. "Look under my bed, Grannie Island and Granma Mainland!"

Oh! What oohs! and aahs! came forth from the two Grandmothers when they opened their handkerchief- and towel-wrapped presents. And what a party they had as well.

There was more to come. Katie Morag looked forward to giving her other presents to the two Grandmothers when the boat came in. And then going to Grannie Island's island party! The Day of the Birthdays just went on and on, thanks to the boat not coming in... It was quite wonderful!

And if the boat doesn't come in ever again, Katie Morag won't worry.
She will always be able to make presents for all of her family and friends.

SPRING

AUTUMN

SUMMER

WINTER